ONE LITTLE GIRL

ONE LITTLE GIRL

by

Joan Fassler

illustrated by M. Jane Smyth

HUMAN SCIENCES PRESS
A Division of Behavioral Publications, Inc.

New York

NEW JUVENILE SERIES ON THE *EXCEPTIONAL CHILD*

Titles

by Phyllis Gold	PLEASE DON'T SAY HELLO
by Edna S. Levine, Ph.D., Litt.D.	LISA AND HER SOUNDLESS WORLD
by Joan Fassler, Ph.D.	ONE LITTLE GIRL

CHILDREN'S SERIES ON *PSYCHOLOGICALLY RELEVANT THEMES*

Titles

by Joan Fassler, Ph.D.	ALL ALONE WITH DADDY
	THE MAN OF THE HOUSE
	MY GRANDPA DIED TODAY
	THE BOY WITH A PROBLEM
	DON'T WORRY, DEAR
by Helen S. Arnstein	BILLY AND OUR NEW BABY
by Harriet Wittels and Joan Griesman	THINGS I HATE
by Terry Berger	I HAVE FEELINGS

Review Committee

Leonard S. Blackman, Ph.D.
Teachers College, Columbia University

Gerald Caplan, M.D.
Harvard Medical School

Eli M. Bower, Ed.D.
University of California, Berkeley

Series Editor:
Sheldon R. Roen, Ph.D.

Copyright 1969 by Behavioral Publications, Inc.
72 Fifth Avenue, New York, N.Y. 10011

Production by Bob Vari

Manufactured in the United States of America

Library of Congress Catalog Card Number 76-80120

ISBN: 0-87705-008-2

Second Printing

For my friend,
Dorothy Stone

Laurie was the first child on her whole
block to run outside and touch the new
white snow.

Laurie was the first child at the beach
to run down to the shore and wriggle her
toes in the wet sand.

Laurie was the first child to hear the robin's chirp in the springtime. And she was the very first child in her whole class to notice a tiny flower pushing up from under the ground.

But the grown-ups said that Laurie was
a slow child. And that made Laurie feel a
little bit bad inside.

But it didn't stop Laurie from being fast at all kinds of interesting things.

She was fast at jumping rope. She could jump 67 times in one minute without missing once. And that, I am sure you know, is pretty fast jumping.

She was fast at brushing her hair. She could brush 130 strokes in less than two minutes — even though her hair was long and wavy. And that, I am sure you know, is pretty fast brushing.

But still the grown-ups said that Laurie was a slow child. And that still made Laurie feel rather bad inside.

Now the truth is that when she was in school, Laurie *was* slow at many things. She was slow at her reading. She was slow at writing her name. She was especially slow when she did the arithmetic problems in her work book. And it often took her a long time to understand what the teacher was telling the class. Sometimes she didn't understand at all.

One morning Laurie heard her teacher say, "Laurie is a slow child." And that, of course, made Laurie feel especially bad inside.

Then one day Laurie's mother took her to a special kind of doctor. The doctor sat Laurie down at a small table. And he gave her games to play. And he asked her to draw a circle. And a square. And a diamond. And he asked her to string some beads and do some puzzles. And he gave her pictures to look at. And he asked her questions about the pictures. And he wrote down *every* single thing that Laurie said. Then Laurie and her mother went home.

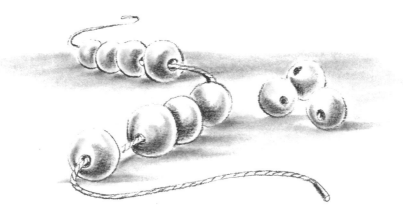

A few days later Laurie's school got a letter from the doctor. And Laurie's mother got a letter from the doctor, too.

Laurie's mother opened the letter quickly and read it through to the end. After a while, she looked up and smiled softly. Then she folded the letter carefully and put it away. But she thought about the letter for a long, long time. And she thought about what the letter said.

And the letter went something like this:

Laurie is a little bit slow at some things. Laurie is a little bit fast at other things. But most important of all, Laurie seems quite happy to be herself.

And somehow, after that day, Laurie noticed something strange. She noticed that many of the grown-ups in her life seemed to change.

Now they began to pay a whole lot more attention to the things that she could do especially well, instead of always worrying about the things she couldn't do very well at all.

Now they began to give Laurie a chance
to really be herself.

Now they stopped saying, "Laurie is a slow child." At least, *mostly* they did. And they began to find many other interesting things to say about Laurie.

And if you think that these simple changes made Laurie feel a little bit better, you are rather wise yourself. Because they certainly did!

In fact, they helped so much that Laurie began to hold her head just a little bit higher. And Laurie began to grow up feeling not so bad inside after all.